Hattie's Magic Show

HAT TRICKS

A book to share from
Scallywag Press

First published in Great Britain in 2019
by Scallywag Press Ltd, 10 Sutherland Row, London SW1V 4JT
This paperback edition published in 2020

Printed in Malaysia on FSC paper by Tien Wah Press

001

British Library Cataloguing in Publication Data available
ISBN 978–1–912650–25–5

Hattie's Magic Show

HAT TRICKS

Satoshi Kitamura

Scallywag Press Ltd
LONDON

What is this?

It's a rabbit in a hat!

But it's not just *any* rabbit,
and it's not just *any* hat . . .

It's Hattie the Magician
and this is *her* hat!

So welcome, everyone,
to Hattie's magic show!

Abracadabra, katakurico…

What's in the hat?

It's a cat!

What will be next?

Abracadabra, katakurico...

What's in the hat?

It's a squirrel!

Abracadabra, katakurico...

What's in the hat?

It's an **octopus**!

Abracadabra, katakurico...

What's in the hat?

It's a moose!

Abracadabra, katakurico...

What's in the hat?

Why, it's an elephant!

But the elephant is stuck.
Oh, oh, oh, it hurts!

One,
two,
three,

heave…

Kaboompskabara!
All
fall
down!

Surely, by now,
the hat is empty.

But no . . .

WoW! What's in the hat?

It's an entire jungle,
with new friends for everyone!